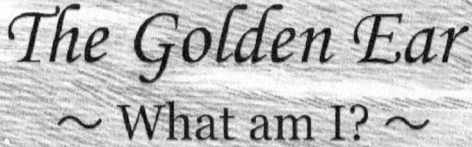

The Golden Ear
~ What am I? ~

Written by Miki Kikkawa

Illustrated by Kunihiko Aoyama

This book was originally published in Japanese under the title
" 金色の耳 " by Parolsha, Tokyo, Japan in 2011.

Author: Miki Kikkawa
Translator: Rieko Sasaki
Illustrator: Kunihiko Aoyama
Coordinator: Junko Rodriguez
Book Designer: Yuko Yoshida

ISBN - 13: 978-09836-40288
ISBN - 10: 0983640289
Babel Corporation
Pacific Business News Bldg. #208,
1833 Kalakaua Avenue,
Honolulu, Hawaii 96815

Phone: (808) 946 - 3773
Fax: (808) 946 - 3993

Website: http://www.bookandright.com/

The Golden Ear

~ What am I? ~

Dedicated to

Rika

who was born with

beautifully shaped ears.

The artistry of nature

inspired me

and

guided me

in the writing of this story.

Prologue - The Legendary Bud

In the days of old, when I was a child, I was shown a very strange drawing.

A long stem grew and stretched out of the water. At the very top of the stem, just one bud was hanging down and facing the water.

I felt strange because the bud was far too long, as long as the stem. It almost reached the surface of the water. There were no leaves, not even one.

Then one day, I was told that the bud was called *The Legendary Bud*.

"This drawing is only about one long bud. But when it's open, it will turn out to be an unusual mystical flower that no one has ever seen before."

I was also told,

"Many people have been looking for this flower for a long time. Some people say somebody has

already found it. But others say nobody has found it yet."

When I heard this story, I was convinced that this strange looking bud had captured the hearts of many people. I felt there was something very mysterious about the bud.

(What kind of flower will it be?)

In my mind's eye, I could see the shape, color, and each petal of the flower. It must have a gorgeous shine such as I had never ever seen before. My imaginings went on and on and on.

Time passed and after a long while, I was told that the bud turned out to be *The Flower who learned who she is*.

The Flower who learned who she is? What does it mean?

"There was a story of before she turned into the flower."

What do you think happened to the bud? What do you think the flower really learned?

The Frog

It was on the mystic marsh.

The water surface was beautifully reflecting the sky like a mirror.

One day, a thin slight stem was growing out of the water.

A frog sitting on a lotus leaf looked at it and murmured.

"Something is growing··· What is it? Is it a reed? Or some sort of a stick?"

The voice of the frog echoed across the water surface and also went up and spread throughout the entire sky. His voice was carried to every aspect endlessly.

But there was one exception. The thin slight stem could not hear the voice of the frog at all.

As you guessed, yes···, The Flower had been born as a stem.

The Water Strider

After a short while, one winding bud sprouted from the thin slight stem.

The bud went stretched down and down until its head almost touched the water mirror. It looked strange, but very delicate and lovely.

A water strider nearby came across and looked at the bud.

"What? I've never seen something like this before! It is a bud. So···, is this a flower? Excuse me, what are you?"

At this point, The Flower who was a hard bud started being able to hear. She was surprised by the very first question that she had heard from others.

(Uh··· "What are you?" ··· I think I am supposed to be a stem. Well, a bud grew out from me today. So···, that means I thought I am a stem who has

grown a bud. It's not true? But as he questioned, I
am ⋯ I am what?)

It was the first time for The Flower with the long,
strange looking bud to be conscious about herself.

The Snowflake

Since The Flower had been questioned by the water strider, she wondered and thought about what she is.

"The more I think, the more I wonder··· What am I really?"

A while later,

from the sky, snowflakes like peony flowers silently fell on an expanse of the water mirror. In a short moment, all around was covered by the snow and was transformed into the purest white world. The snowflakes fell on top of The Flower's long thin bud. They started clinging to its stem as well.

"Wow···, it's so white and so cool."

While feeling the cool whiteness, The Flower was somehow inspired and wanted to ask one of the snowflakes what she is.

"Excuse me, Snowflake. I would like to know what I am. What do you think I am?"

The snowflake answered.

"I think···, you are a flower although you look like a bud right now. But actually, I think the correct answer is you are *a traveler*."

"*A traveler?*"

"Yes, for example, I am snow, a snowflake shaped like a peony flower right now. But soon I will melt and disappear. I will become water, then vapor···, and I will go up into the sky and become a cloud. All living things are always changing at every little moment including now. Nothing stays in the same form in this world. That is why I think you are also *a traveler*. You are changing your form while travelling through time and space."

The snowflake's words seemed to speak to The Flower, but also seemed to speak to the snowflake herself. The Flower was amazed by her words.

The snowflake shone with reflected light from the sun and added more in her pure voice.

"I am sure that you will understand this in the near future. All things are changing without exception. This is fleeting, sad, and full of sorrow ⋯, yes, this is. But listen, even if it is so, you will surely understand someday how wonderful it is and how many blessings it has. I promise."

In the beautiful sunlight, the snowflake slowly and imperceptibly melted, and then completely disappeared. No trace was left at all.

The Crescent Moon

Up in the sky, the crescent moon surrounded by white fog was shining down on the purest white world. He was watching and listening to the whole scene below.

The Flower was repeating '*a traveler*' in her mind. But she did not feel fully satisfied with the snow-flake's words. She still wondered what she is.

On that night, the silvery water mirror was illuminated by bright light from the crescent moon. A most mystic silence was all around the marsh. The Flower lifted up her long hanging bud toward the crescent moon. She looked up at the silvery moonlight dreamily in the godly quietness.

One thought came to her mind. She decide to ask the crescent moon, too "what she is."

"By bathing in your light, everything glows silver. By bathing in your light, I feel very spiritual. Crescent Moon, I have something to ask you··· I was told that I am *a traveler*. I was also told that all

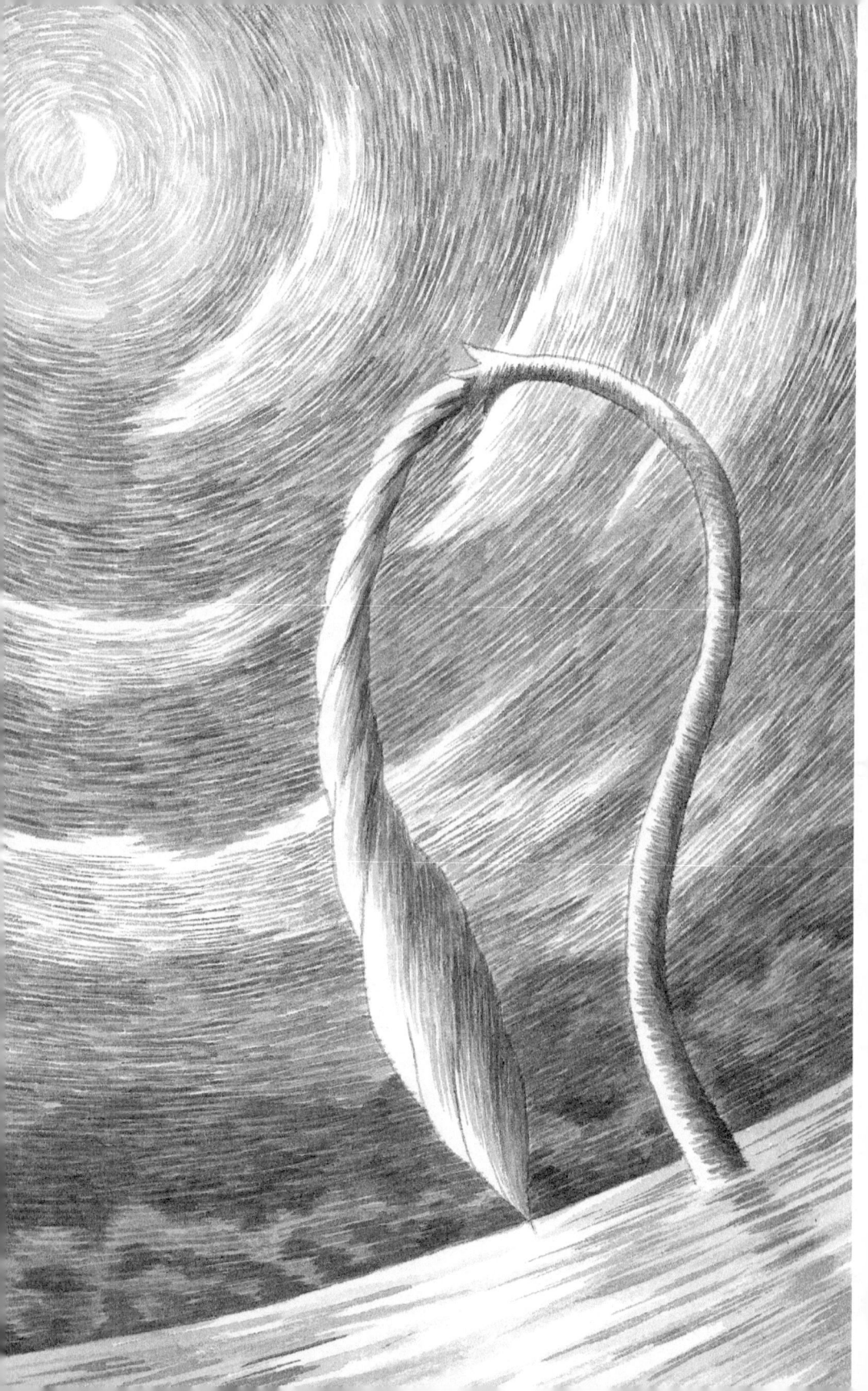

things are *travelers*. When you look at me in your silvery moonlight, what do you think I am?"

In response to this question, the crescent moon glowed more brightly - it was hard to tell if its light was silver or gold - and he answered in a young fresh voice.

"Oh yes, *a traveler*... I hadn't thought about that. Yes, you surely are *a traveler*. So am I. But I think you are a *rhythm*, too. A *rhythm* that goes up and down. A *rhythm* you made by yourself. I feel all things are *rhythm*s each played by itself. Well, I think you can say you are *a traveler* and also a *rhythm*."

"*A rhythm*? One going up and down? And my own *rhythm*?"

The crescent moon gently let a much clearer light fall down all over The Flower's bud and stem, and spoke again.

"That's correct. You know···, I have a reason for feeling like that. In fact, I never ever increase nor decrease. It is just the perceptions of those looking at me from the ground. At first, I was wondering. I am neither increasing nor decreasing, but why does everyone on the ground call me 'the crescent moon' or 'the full moon'? That was my question. But one day I figured it out. There must be a reason. I must be playing my own role. Then I thought like this. By appearing as if I am increasing or decreasing each day, I might represent that life is *rhythm* to all other things."

The crescent moon continued.

"You are the same. I am the same. All things are the same. We all have time to make increasing *rhythm* but also time to make decreasing *rhythm*. There is nothing that just keeps only increasing or only decreasing. When I look down at everything on the ground, I cannot help thinking about this. Each one of them is playing a long unique music through its life by making its own *rhythm*."

"Life··· That is *rhythm*."

The Flower murmured. And she focused both on her stem and bud for the first time to feel her own *rhythm* in her body.

The crescent moon whispered gently to her while bathing the whole snowy world with an even clearer silvery light.

"Someday, you will be impressed about 'what a wonderful *rhythm* each of us has.' You will surely be impressed. Well, Flower, your *rhythm* is also very marvelous. Very···"

The Sun

The next morning,

The water mirror that had shone with the silvery moonlight was sparkling under the bright sunshine.

The Flower received its brilliant light and felt full of energy. Then her long winding bud swelled slightly as it warmed up in the gentle light.

"How nice and warm. It feels so peaceful... And how shiny it is. I can't believe that I have encountered something like this, so warm and comfortable."

The Flower thought that the sun might know the answer to her most important question "what she is" because it has the power to send such a bright light from a far high place. So she asked the sun.

"Hello, Sun. I have something to ask you. You are in a very high place and sending us such a brilliant light, so I think you know the answer. Uh⋯,

what do you think I am?"

The sun answered in a powerful warm sunny voice.

"You are a flower. Now you are a bud, though... But I don't think you are just a bud or a flower because you have *something* that supports you. That *something* is the one being always with you. First of all, without that *something*, you cannot live as a flower. You are actually living while being one with *something* that is working for you. That *something* is inexpressibly *amazing, great, and precious*. That is why you are a flower. But at the same time, you - yourself - are also *something amazing, great, and precious*."

"I am a flower as well as *something amazing, great, and precious*. How wonderful!"

The sun's words surprised The Flower. The Flower looked very pure and fresh. The sun felt The

Flower was adorable and said some more.

"I am sure that everyone would feel like me if they were looking at things from a far distance. Even for you, you will surely understand this someday.

"For mountains, for seas, for marshes, for trees, for grasses, for winds··· as well as for all things being there, there is *something* that is working for and supporting them. Don't you think so? If that *something amazing, great, and precious* was not working, how could the mountains be so stately as they are? How could the seas make such elegant waves? How could the marsh have a mystic atmosphere and even embrace so many creatures? How could the trees keep standing refreshingly and watching the flow of time? Even for you, if that *something* was not working for you, how could you be so lively?

"And you know what···? Even for me, there is *something* that is working for me. I know this. That is why

I can be very calm and peaceful. *Something* is always supporting me, protecting me, and embracing me. *Something* is always being with me and working for me.

"In the near future, you will understand that 'all things are with *something amazing, great, and precious*.' Someday, you will understand this very well and deeply in your heart."

During this conversation between The Flower and the sun, everything including The Flower and surroundings was basking in the shine from the sun. They were all sparkling beautifully.

"By the way, Flower, why don't you look at yourself - your form - in the water mirror now?"

The Flower looked at herself in the surface of the water where there were no ripples but just a smooth clear mirror.

And what happened? The Flower noticed her bud

was swelling even more.

"Something is working for me⋯ *Something amazing, great, and precious.* I am a *traveler.* I am *rhythm*⋯"

The Flower murmured while looking at herself reflecting in the water mirror of the marsh.

The Seahorse

After several days, something else happened on the marsh.

On the surface of the water mirror, the face of a rare fish called a 'seahorse' popped up. As it was a very strange looking fish, The Flower was surprised and could not help asking.

"Ah⋯ Excuse me, what are you?"

In response to this question, the strange looking creature jumped up from the water and tumbled in the air to show his whole body.

"I am a seahorse! I am a fish, but my face and head look like a horse with a mane. And my lower body is like a fish. You know, I wanted to be born as a horse. But⋯, although I look like a horse, I was somehow born as a fish."

"A seahorse⋯"

To The Flower, it was totally an unfamiliar name.

His unusual looking face and head were also un-familiar to her. She took a long look at his body and repeated his name over and over again.

"Seahorse···, seahorse···, seahorse···"

On the other hand, the seahorse himself was also surprised with The Flower because of her unusual looking long bud that was almost touching the water surface. The seahorse had never ever seen such a thing before.

"I know I look unusual. But so you do··· What are you really?"

The seahorse asked The Flower. Then The Flower replied shyly.

"I am···, I am a bud but also a flower··· But I re-ally don't know. Seahorse, when you look at me what do you think I am?"

This question made the seahorse think that this

strange looking flower might be distressed with something just like he used to be.

"Hmm…, if I'm correct, you wanted to be born as something else, right? Well it's okay. You don't need to say so. I know how you feel because I wanted to be born as something else, too. A horse! So I can understand exactly how you feel. No wonder because of your strange looking… Oops! Sorry, no, I mean you are unique. So unique!"

The Flower felt hurt. The seahorse told The Flower that she looks 'strange' face-to-face. She was worried. Other things that she had met such as the snowflake, the crescent moon or the sun, they might also have felt the same thing.

"Everyone told me like I am *a traveler*, *rhythm*, or *something amazing, great, and precious*. But they might be just trying to be nice and make me cheer up because I look very strange."

The Flower became more and more depressed.

However, the seahorse didn't look like he cared very much about how she felt. He kept telling her jokingly but seriously.

"Listen, I was also having a hard time. That's why I know what your problem is. By the way, don't misunderstand about me. I don't look like it, but I am actually able to figure out who is good at listening and understanding. I know you are. So okay, this is the story just between you and me.

"One day, I heard a mysterious voice. A very mysterious voice. I think the voice was probably from the marsh spirit. It was an absolutely astounding experience. At that time, from out of nowhere, I heard a hoarse voice echo through the whole marsh. That voice told me this.

"'You, Dearest Seahorse, you were not born as a seahorse by accident.'

"Did you hear that? He said 'Dearest' to me. 'Dearest!' I felt I was so special! Anyway, the voice told me this;

"'You exist as *the result of every cause and effect as well as the virtue and great compassion* that have all accumulated from the very far distant past in perfect balance and harmony.'

"Well, at first, I couldn't understand. *Cause and effect? Virtue? Compassion? Accumulated?* I didn't get any of it at all. I just wanted to be a horse dashing through the grassland while swinging my shiny mane. But the fact is I am living in this weird marsh. And I look so awkward. Don't be kidding! That's what I first thought about his words.

"But you know what? Life is interesting. One understanding came into my head. I think people call it a 'revelation.' I actually felt that I had received the words from God. I might have heard something incredible. No, not "might". I actually

did.

"Since then, I've been repeating the marsh spirit's words in my head; 'All things exist as they are for a reason.' 'I am *the result of everything that accumulated from the very far distant past.'* Yup, something like that.

"I still don't know the difficult concepts very well, such as *'cause and effect' 'virtue' or 'compassion.'* But it is amazing. I felt what I heard is all true. Now, I believe that they are the true words that God gave me.

"Anyway, I just thought that I had to share these words somehow. That's why I told you this story."

The seahorse talked about his experience very cheerfully.

Between the seahorse and The Flower, there was the sun right above them. The sun clicked slightly. The seahorse glanced up at the sun.

"Oh no, I forgot my lunchtime. I have to go now. But you know what? Don't tell anybody what I just told you. The marsh spirit talked to me... *Cause and effect, accumulated*... Nobody would believe such a thing. If you tell that, I know I would be called crazy. I am already a crazy looking guy. I don't want anybody talking about me more than now.

"But you are an exception. Okay, you have to keep telling yourself the words that I heard from the marsh spirit. Repeat it many times. And again, repeat it many times day after day. Then someday, you will understand that what I told you is all truth. You will also understand what the marsh spirit was trying to say."

Leaving these words, "See you, bye" the seahorse vigorously jumped into the water and disappeared.

The Flower Queen

The Flower thought.

"I have asked many things 'what am I?' Each one gave me a different answer.

"The snowflake said '*a traveler*.' The crescent moon said 'a *rhythm*.' The seahorse said '*the result of everything that accumulated from the very far distant past*.' Then the sun said '*something amazing, great, and precious*.'

"They do seem very certain. But I am getting more confused. What is the truth? I am··· I am what really?"

Then one day, The Flower noticed a pink large flower on the water mirror of the marsh. She had a bud just like The Flower had. The Flower was excited and immediately spoke to the pink large flower.

"You have a bud just like me, haven't you?"

"What? Just like you? Not at all! I am the Flower Queen. My bud is not like yours. It is not hanging down. It is not unattractive like yours."

The large flower was the flower queen. She was very proud and was righteously offended by what The Flower had said. The Flower was very shocked just like she was when she had first met the seahorse.

"The seahorse told me that I am 'strange.' I knew ⋯ Yes, I knew it⋯"

However, The Flower reminded herself that who she met is the flower queen and thought again.

"Compared to the flower queen, who has an elegant form, I am just an unattractive plant. I know I am. But maybe⋯!"

One idea crossed her mind.

(She is the same flower as me. Even better, she is

the flower queen···Yes! She might know exactly what I am.)

The Flower asked the flower queen.

"Your majesty has a different form from mine, but surely we are in the same group of flowers. Therefore, I would like to ask you one thing. When your majesty looks at me, what do you think? What do you think I am?"

The flower queen thought she had been a bit too harsh on The Flower.

"Ahem." The flower queen cleared her throat.

"Are you asking me what I would think you are? Such an annoying question. But if I were to tell you, I could say···. well, you are *an embodiment of the sunshine, winds, and water*."

"*An embodiment of the sunshine, winds, and water*? Your majesty, what do you mean?"

The flower queen replied.

"What this means is you are made of what you have consumed. You have been absorbing the sunshine, receiving winds, and drinking water. In other words, you have been shaped by the sunshine, the winds, and the water. Thus, you are an embodiment of those things.

"And···, yes, this one too. Take a look at this butterfly drinking my nectar."

The Flower leaned forward and took a close look into the petals of the flower queen. As the flower queen said, a little butterfly was eagerly drinking her nectar.

"What a lovely butterfly!"

"Ahem!" The flower queen cleared her throat again even louder. Then she spoke to The Flower in a haughty tone.

"You are very rude. You know in nature, in order to talk to me - The Flower Queen -, you are required to request an audience. Moreover, you must ask my permission before you are allowed to converse with me. Well, I can say today is special, though···"

The flower queen glared at The Flower and continued.

"Based on the story I just told you, what do you think this butterfly is the embodiment of?

"Yes, it is supposed to be an embodiment of nectar. Then, how about my nectar? In order to become nectar, the nectar required sunshine, winds, air, water, and many other things. Therefore, the nectar is an embodiment of sunshine, winds, air, water, and many other things. If you followed this story to go back and further back, what is going to happen? After all, do you think each one contains all the things in this universe?"

Then the flower queen said,

"All things exist by being given life from others. One life is supported by, inherited from, and consists of many other lives. Those other lives also provide their lives to make the lives of others better.

"Listen, someday you will see yourself with your flower blooming and reflected in this water mirror. At that time, I am sure that you will remember what I said. Then, you will surely think, 'Yes, this is exactly what the flower queen told me. Inside of me, there are so many other things living.'"

When the flower queen finished, she shook her large petals proudly.

"The flower queen is a bit peculiar, but she told me something very unexpected."

The Flower looked at all of herself in the water

mirror.

"This stem, this bud swelling every single day – when I really think about it, it is made of various lives from the whole wide world, including the sunshine, winds, air, water, and many other things."

The Flower realized that and remembered about the snowflake.

(Yes, the snowflake told me "I am snow, a snowflake shaped like a peony flower right now. But soon I will melt and disappear. I will become water, then vapor⋯, and I will go up into the sky and become a cloud." She said something like this. I am actually drinking water and taking in vapor as well⋯ It means the water I have drunk might be the water that used to be the snowflake. If so, I am an embodiment of the snowflake, too! The snowflake is still living in my body!)

From this day, The Flower was filled with a sense

of affinity with all things including the air, water, and winds.

The Oak Leaf

The next day, The Flower was still looking at herself reflecting in the water mirror of the marsh.

Then she noticed that the tip of her swelling bud had started blooming little by little. The Flower was very thrilled.

"When it blooms, what kind of flower will it be?"

However…

Her excitement didn't last long. The Flower was very shocked by something she just noticed. It was as if she had been struck by lightning.

In fact, The Flower had wondered for a long time. She had had that question together with another question of "what am I?" While looking at herself slowly shaking on the water mirror, The Flower noticed what was missing for her.

"I had thought something was missing for a long time. Now I know it!"

Yes, it was 'leaves.'

The Flower had a swelling bud, but she had no leaves. Not even one. What she had was only a long unattractive bud. The Flower fully understood.

(The seahorse called me 'strange.' So had the flower queen, too⋯ Now I know what they meant.)

While The Flower was thinking that, she looked at a big tree. Its branches stretched above the marsh. When she took a further look, she noticed that the tree was fully covered by many lively leaves shaking in the breeze. It was just like the leaves were singing together.

"Why not⋯, why don't I have leaves?" The Flower sadly murmured.

Then, there was a voice coming from somewhere.

"For those who don't have leaves, they are totally okay as they are. You are fulfilling your own role. This world consists of divided tasks. Each one has its own role. We all play our own role to support this world. That's why you do not need to feel sad about such a thing."

The voice seemed to be from an oak leaf. The Flower felt she was encouraged by his words.

"Oak Leaf, you are so sweet. Your words make me so relieved. 'For those who don't have leaves, they are totally okay as they are.' How wonderful!

"Well···, could I ask you one thing? To tell the truth, I have had something I really wanted to know but I have not figured it out yet. That is the question of 'what am I?' Oak Leaf, what do you think about me?"

While comfortably rustling in the winds, the oak leaf answered.

"You are ⋯ You are surely an unusual flower with no leaves. But you know, I think you are one of the varieties of individualities that are present in this universe. To me, it seems to be like this. You are *representing this universe with your own individuality*."

"Are you sure? I am *representing this universe with my own individuality*?"

"That's right. Let me explain some more. The universe expresses what it is supposed to be with one's individuality. The universe shows what the universe is by your existence. Your individuality shows the universe itself. This applies to all other things. The universe expresses itself through all things.

"One day, you will certainly enjoy being yourself more than now. You will understand how valuable your individuality is, how shiny and glorious all other things are with their irreplaceable individualities, and how beautiful this universe is, full of all those individualities."

The warm and thoughtful words from the oak leaf made The Flower feel fully energized.

"The flower with no leaves – that is absolutely myself."

The Flower started to feel so.

The Rice Plant

Since the day that The Flower talked to the oak leaf, she had been feeling more confident about herself. At the same time, she was able to see things around her with her new vision.

It was one of those days. The Flower saw spectacular scenery over the water mirror of the marsh. It was the beautiful sight of rice plants.

Now The Flower could speak in a more mature manner. And also she had grown and become taller. That is why she was able to notice things over the marsh that she had not seen before. The Flower used to think that the things on the water mirror and the sky above her were all that there was in this world. But now she found that the actual world was much larger and extended further beyond the marsh than she had thought.

The world of the rice plants was just like a world of gold. It was brilliantly shining. It was absolute ethereal beauty.

The Flower was admiring the beautiful scenery. And somehow, the words of the oak leaf came to her mind – *the beauty representing the universe*. Simultaneously, she remembered the words of the sun – *something amazing, great, and precious*. The scene of the rice plants was exactly as described by such words.

"How beautiful⋯ And how godly⋯"

The Flower was taking deep breaths of admiration over and over again. While doing so, she started to feel like asking "what she is" to the rice plants as well.

"Such golden shiny rice plants, I wonder how they would answer my question."

The Flower almost asked. But she noticed that the rice plants were far beyond the marsh. It didn't seem that her voice could reach them even if she spoke very loudly. The Flower was disappointed.

(Rice Plants, you are unbelievably godly and beautiful. I wanted to ask you something. I just wanted to ask you what you would think I am···, but···)

Then, an amazing thing happened.

From somewhere, whispers responded to The Flower. It was a very small voice.

"Well, you are a flower. A flower that has no leaves. So it's a bit of an unusual type. But you are not an existence that is recognized as a flower only by your appearance. For example, in each of my tiny little grains of rice, *there is the world of infinity*. You are the same. *There is the world of infinity in your body, too*. You are the existence embracing a vast universe inside you that is as enormous as the wide world outside of you. This applies to all things. For each one of us, *there is a vast universe with infinity inside us*."

Surprisingly, the voice was from the rice plant. The whispers continued.

"I just told you that *'there is the world of infinity.'* But in other words, I could also say that the universe is condensed in each of my tiny little grains of rice. Look at your roots. Even in a drop of the water mirror, the universe is condensed in there. Not just about you, for all things, *the vast universe is broadening in each one of us and the vast universe is condensed in each one of us.*"

Listening to the rice plant, The Flower felt as if she was broadening further and further limitlessly. At the same time, she felt as if she was shrinking smaller and smaller endlessly.

Again, the rice plant whispered.

"In the universe broadening limitlessly in your body, an enormous number of memories are engraved. Now, inside you being right now and right there, all things of the universe are embraced. Inside the you of now, there are a colossal number of memories and legacies from the very far distant past. Inside the you of now, there are the

seeds of hope for the future. They are all inside of you now."

The Winds

Since talking to the rice plant, The Flower had enjoyed the sensation of broadening limitlessly and shrinking endlessly.

But one question just came to her mind.

(At that time, I was first talking to myself only in my mind. I didn't say any words. But why? Why could I talk to the rice plant?)

The Flower's question was so strong. Her internal voice became waves and echoed across the sky "Why? Why? Why?..."

How amazing! A mystical thing occurred.

Very gentle winds blew around The Flower. They started singing in response to her question.

> ♪ *That's because*
> *You are resonating with all things.*
> *All things are resonating with each other.*

Resonating means calling.
Even if there are no voices or no sounds can be heard,
With silent voices, with silent sounds,
It is all calling one another.

And you know,
Lives calling one another means
Lives influencing one another.

Even between two separate huge continents.
Even between the surface of the ocean that winds can gently touch and
The very dark depths of the ocean that winds will never be able to meet.
Yes, even to the end of the universe.

Pleasure, crying, or sadness of each life,
They are all communicating with each other.
Regardless of being known by someone else or not.

They are connecting with each other deeply and deeply.
That is the wonder of life. ♪

While singing the song, the winds gently swung the bud of The Flower and passed by.

After listening to the song by the winds, The Flower somehow felt so light and refreshed.

"Yes⋯ I understand now⋯ I am *resonating and connecting with all things*⋯"

The Star

Several days passed.

At night under a sky full of stars, The Flower was thinking about the things she had met and talked with, one by one.

The snowflake, the crescent moon, the sun, the seahorse, the flower queen, the oak leaf, the rice plant, the winds ⋯

Then, one of the stars sent a ray of light toward the water mirror of the marsh. The light beamed into The Flower's swelling bud.

The star started talking calmly and softly in a low husky voice to The Flower.

"You have been asking many things 'what you are,' right? I was watching you all the time from the sky. You really want to know what you are, don't you? Well, if I could answer your question, I would say⋯ you are ⋯ *an eternal life and soul.*

"You know···, *life and soul* is something that never ends. It is something that is never completed either. To tell the truth, I will be a shooting star tonight and leave this life. As a star, I will end my life. However, it doesn't mean this is the end of *my real life and soul*. I will keep living even after I die. It must be hard for you to believe it, but I will keep living even after I disappeared in my form as a star. That's because *our lives and souls are eternal*. There is no concept of beginning or ending in our *lives and souls*. Being born and dying. Dying and being born again. Being born is miracle. Dying is also miracle. *The life and soul* repeats its mystery."

The Flower listened to the star that will be a shooting star and leave his life on that night. Then she remembered the words of the snowflake.

(The snowflake told me I am *a traveler*. Maybe, it also meant I am *a traveler of life and soul* who repeats being born and dying eternally. All beings are travelers who change their forms and states from moment to moment in their lives, but also are eternal travelers who repeat being born and dying…)

Just on time when The Flower thought that, a stream of light drew an arc and soon disappeared.

The Flower felt tears come to her eyes. The tears rolled down into the water mirror of the marsh. As it happened, up in the sky very far from her, a newborn star twinkled.

The Mountain

The tip of The Flower's bud was almost about to open. The whole bud was swelling more and nicely packed like a ball. The thin slight stem and the really big bud – it certainly looked odd and funny. That form wouldn't be familiar to anybody.

At the same time, The Flower had grown more. She was tall enough, and one day, she could see the far off range of mountains. Across the water mirror of the marsh, the rice plants were shining gold and gently swinging side to side. Beyond the rice plants, the mountains sat solidly. The Flower felt something very dependable while looking at those mountains.

"How stately they are⋯"

As usual, The Flower felt like asking the mountains as well.

(They look so calm, solid, and composed. They are fully covered by dark blackish greens. They look like they are guarding the whole area. I have

to ask the mountains 'what I am.' And I know the distance doesn't matter to communicate.)

The Flower spoke toward the far off mountains in her mind.

(Hello, Mountains. When someone solid like you looks at me, what do you think? What do you think I am?)

In response to her question, she heard an old man's reply with a gentle laugh.

"Apparently, all beings seem that they cannot help exploring what they are. So, maybe I could say that all beings are the ones who cannot help studying what they are. Ha, ha, ha..."

It was from the oldest mountain. He continued to talk while laughing openly and generously.

"In other words, I can say 'you are *the one who is trying to get better and better*'. Whether be-

ing aware of it or not, all things are supposed to improve themselves infinitely. All things have an automatic control system in their bodies to be better and better. Therefore, I have to say you are *the one who is trying to get better and better.*"

The Flower listened to these words. She again looked at the range of mountains admiringly.

"It was very encouraging. Just like how they look, everything he told me was really reliable and big-hearted..."

The Big Hawk, The Small Fish, and
The Marsh Spirit

A few days later, something seemed to be different.

It was a day when the water mirror of the marsh was sparkling brightly. In the delightful sunshine, The Flower was looking at the sky as well as watching the surface of the water mirror.

Up in the sky, a big hawk was flying. Right under the water surface, a small fish was swimming. The Flower alternately and intently looked at both the big hawk and the small fish. She then closed her eyes and absorbedly listened to the sounds that the hawk and the fish were making.

The Flower felt as if her entire body turned out to be an ear. She could feel the big hawk wheeling in the sky. She could even clearly hear the voice of the hawk soaring grandly in the sky.

"For me flying in the sky, the sky is my life. It is everything to me. I am looking down on the marsh, mountains, rice plants, and human beings

– I am looking down at everything from this sky while gliding freely. How pleasant to feel this. How wonderful to fly around. How wonderful to soar freely. And how wonderful to be alive!"

The Flower kept closing her eyes. She could also feel the small fish swimming right under the water surface. She could even clearly hear its voice in the water.

"For me swimming in the water, the water is my life. It is everything to me. I am swimming in the water. How pleasant to feel this. How wonderful to swim around. And how wonderful to be alive!"

The Flower could listen to their joyful voices with her ear-like body. She could then even listen to the voice of the marsh spirit.

"There are no fish that have left the water. There are no birds that have left the sky. For fish, the water is their lives. For birds, the sky is their lives. It is so as you just have heard in your heart.

I am sure that you will be able to listen to the other silent voices of many other things more and more. And eventually, someday, you will fully understand. *The earth where you are now is your life itself. The whole universe is your life itself.* You will surely and deeply understand this."

Then one thought ran through The Flower's mind.

"These words⋯ I feel like I have heard them a long time ago. I feel rather nostalgic. It's like I just remembered something that I had already known before, a very long time ago⋯"

Then, she found an amazingly mystical thing on the water mirror.

"Oh!!"

The day finally came.

(Something like a butterfly wing is open on top of the thin slight stem! It's shining in Gold⋯ It's me!)

The water mirror was showing The Flower herself who came fully into bloom. It was a big flower. It was a mystical form. And it gave off the radiance of Gold.

The Flower held her breath. She kept looking into herself in the water mirror. Then the big hawk wheeling above and watching her shouted loudly. It was as loud as if his voice could shake the whole universe.

"That flower is an Ear! It is exactly same as the Ear of a human being! I have seen this before!"

His shout was carried by winds and echoed through on the mountains. It reverberated through all aspects endlessly.

The Flower heard the voice filled the whole universe. And she exclaimed happily and joyfully,

"Ah⋯, now I understand. I am The Ear! I am The Ear Flower! I am The Golden-colored Ear Flower

that is able to listen to all things in this universe!"

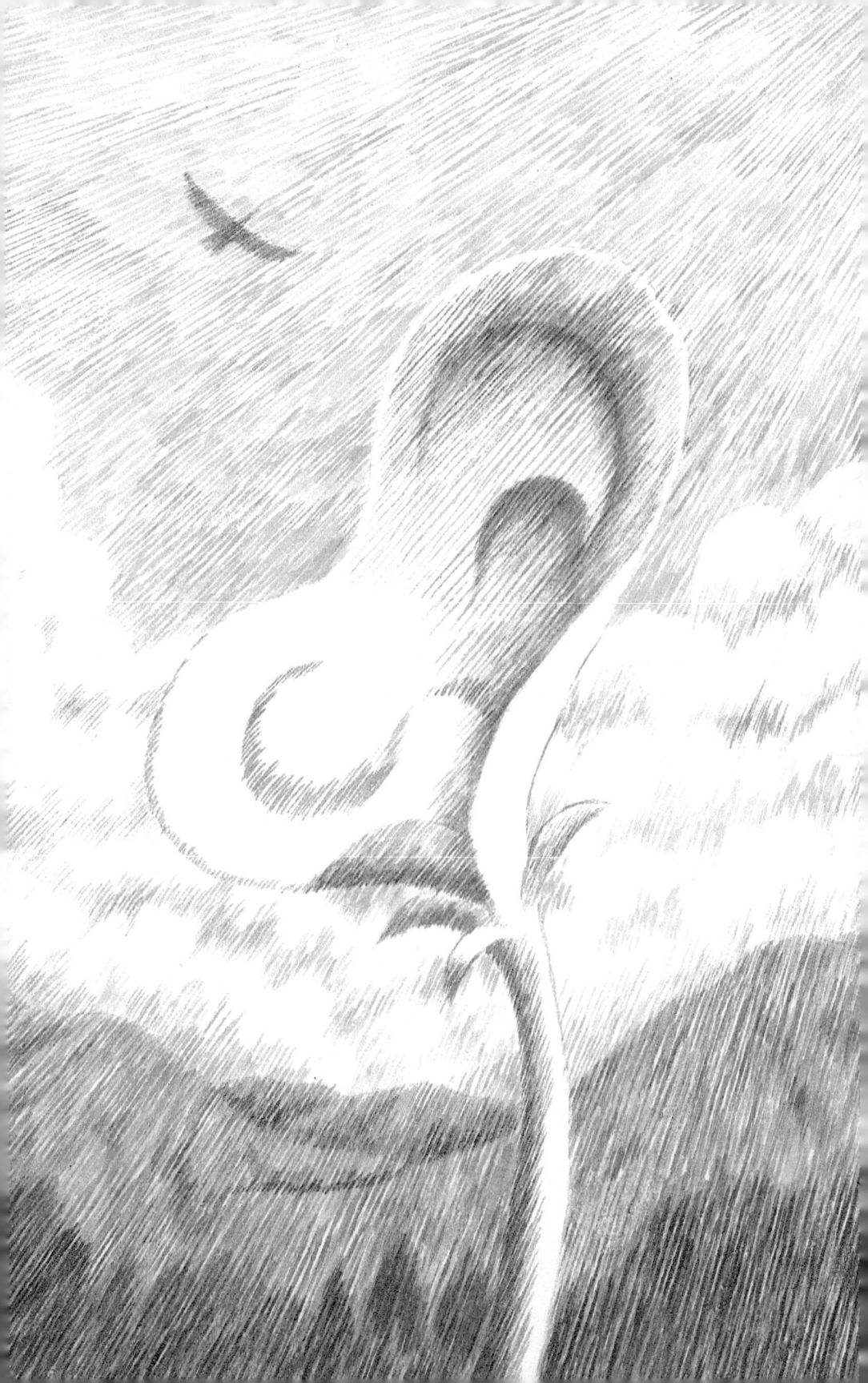

Epilogue - The Water Mirror

Now let me tell you what had happened after The Flower learned that she was The Ear Flower.

One day, The Ear Flower unintentionally glanced down her root. Then, a great sensation flashed in her heart. She was impressed by something that had always been around her, but she had never ever seen before consciously.

How brilliantly beautiful the water mirror is! The Ear Flower noticed it for the very first time.

"Hello, Water Mirror!"

She right away spoke to the water mirror.

"I have always been so close to you, but until now, I haven't noticed how beautiful you are… What have I seen so far? You are absolutely clear, pure, and shining as far as the eye can see. You have no turbidity at all."

The water mirror responded gently and softly.

"I am the water mirror. But when gentle winds blow and rub my body, very small waves are made. At that time, I will be the gentle wind. When a storm comes and shakes my body, big rough waves are made. At that time, I will be the storm. When there is no wind, I will be the water mirror with the ultimate quietness.

"When the silent water mirror is made, there the sky is shown, the floating clouds are shown, the flying birds are shown, and the moon is shown. At each time, I am not only the water mirror, but also the sky, the clouds, the birds, and the moon. There is no gap or border between the sky, the clouds, the birds, the moon, and me. I am each of them. I will be the sky, and the sky will be me. I will be the birds, and the birds will be me.

"You told me that I am absolutely clear, pure, and shining as far as the eye can see. You also told me that I have no turbidity at all. This will happen when something becomes extremely pure. When there are no dark thoughts but just the innocent and pure mind exists, what will happen? I am expressing its answer by my appearance as the water mirror. This is the ultimate form when things are the very purest.

"You have asked many things 'what you are.' The fact is, *when you attained absolute purity, you can be anything in this world.* You are an existence having unlimited potential."

Said the water mirror.

"It's hard for me now to imagine, but I think it must be so. This world is really mystical···"

The Ear Flower murmured. Then the water mirror said to her softly and quietly.

"You are Me, I am You···"

~ To be continued ~

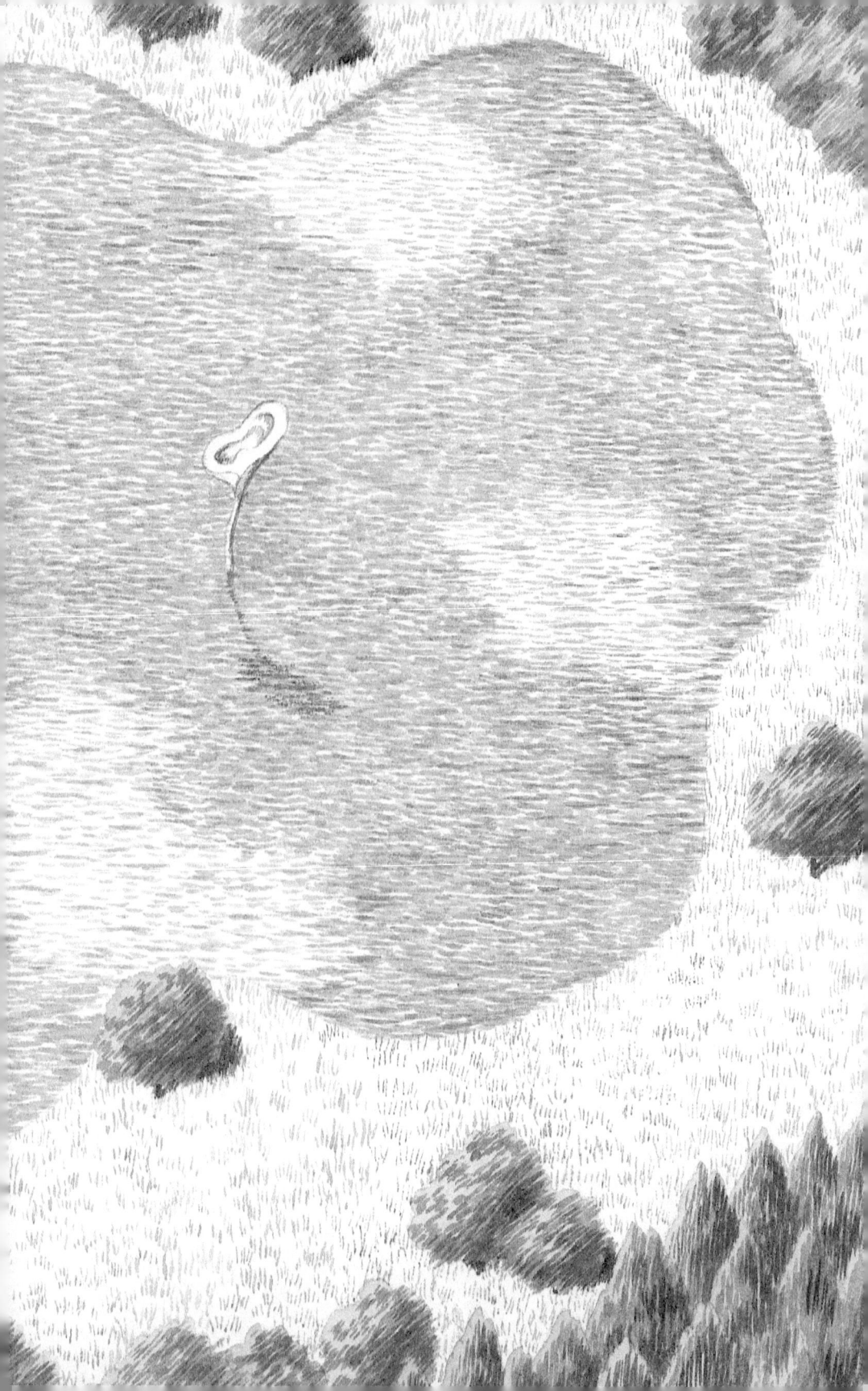

About the Author

Miki Kikkawa is an award-winning author, public speaker, business owner, and lecturer at the University of Niigata Prefecture as well as a school board member for the Niigata Prefecture in Japan.

She was born in 1966 and grew up with the influence of her family's tradition of Zen Buddhism. She studied educational psychology at Osaka Kyoiku University. Upon graduation from the school, she worked at the human resources department at Kobe Steel, Ltd. After marriage, she moved to one of the historic castle towns, Murakami City in Niigata.

In 1988, she started involving herself in various projects to promote and boost the development of the Murakami City together with her husband, Shinji Kikkawa, who had been appointed as one of the members of *Kanko Karisuma* (The Special Tourism Promoters) by the Japan Cabinet Office and the Japan Tourism Agency in the Ministry of Land, Infrastructure, Transport, and Tourism.

Their continuous activities and energetic efforts have been highly awarded and acknowledged. They have received various awards including the Japan Prime Minister Award and the Tiffany Foundation Award.

Kikkawa also wrote a story for a TV documentary program in 2003. This work won the Murakami City Award as well as the Memorial Document Award of the 50th celebration of the start of the Broadcasting System of Niigata (BSN).

She has written the books focused on her life themes of "exploring and reconsidering the radiance of life" and "the revitalization of local town and individualities." Her major works include:

2004 "町屋と人形さまの町おこし *Machiya to ningyosama no machiokoshi*"(Local revitalization with traditional merchant's houses and dolls: in Japanese) Gakugei Shuppansha

2009 "心を育てる　地域・観光・人間力の教育

Kokoro wo sodateru chiiki, kanko, ningenryoku no kyoiku" (Education for local communities, tourism, and humanity to cultivate our minds and spirits: in Japanese) Meijitosho Shuppan; The Special Award of Japan Society of Urban and Regional Planners

2010 " 青い眼をもった木 *Aoi me wo motta ki*" (The Tree with A Blue Eye: in Japanese) Tokyo Tosho Shuppan

2011 " 金色の耳 *Kin no mimi*" (The Golden Ear: in Japanese) Parol Sha
" 青い眼をもった木が見た夢 *Aoi me wo motta ki ga mita yume*" (The Dream of The Tree with A Blue Eye: in Japanese) Tokyo Tosho Shuppan

2012 " 鹿の祈り *Shika no inori*" (The Deer's Prayer: in Japanese) Tokyo Tosho Shuppan

2013 *"The Golden Ear"* (in English) Babel Press

These books were made based on Kikkawa's prac-

tical experiences in her work of local revitalization. What is the most important thing to do to make society energized? Kikkawa had wondered and noticed the key is hidden in each individual, a minimum unit of society. In order to make each person realize one's power, all of their values and potentials - the radiance of life - should be explored and reconsidered. Since Kikkwa noticed this, she has been continuously writing for readers in Japan and now the world. *The Golden Ear"* was translated into English in 2013 as her first non-Japanese book.

For more information, visit her website at http://miki-kikkawa.com/en/

From the Translator

I cannot forget the heartfelt moment when I first read the Japanese original version of this book. "What am I?" "Who am I?" These are the questions that translators have in our jobs writing the words of various people as if we were them. For some translators, this question makes them face the obstacle of their self-identities. I was no exception. I have experienced that kind of feeling. But when I came to the end of the Epilogue of this book, I found the phrases releasing me from my struggle. *"When you attained absolute purity, you can be anything in this world."* "*You are Me. I am You.*" I instantly felt that these words were for me, too.

As a translator, what I provide to you are 'words.' However, they are only a tool. What I really have to convey to you is the author's 'heart and soul.' It may also be described as the author's wisdom and love. In order to provide you with those invisible things, 'words' are very important but not enough. My mind needs to feel emptiness. My mind needs to be at the state of *absolute purity*.

Otherwise, I would not be able to feel the author's heart and soul deeply. Even I could feel them properly, I would not be able to convey them correctly without a mind of pureness. That was what I realized again when I first read this book in Japanese.

After I finished my translating, I had another feeling in my mind as simply just one of the readers. *"Absolute purity"* *"You are Me. I am You."* These might be expressing the importance of 'compassion' and 'loving-kindness' that are needed for all of us towards others but also towards ourselves.

Purify our minds. Purify our surroundings. Purify our eyes to see them. Then, we might be eventually able to understand things correctly, accept them generously, learn a lot from them, act properly, and grow more. I could not help feeling like this at the end.

What I can do is still limited as both a translator and a human. But I sincerely hope that the author's heart and soul had been brought to you through this book along with her kindness, sincerity, and the *absolute purity* that I surely felt from her while communicating with her throughout this translation project.

At last, I would like to express my deepest gratitude to the author Miki Kikkawa and all talented members of the publisher, Babel Press, and Babel Group; Miyoko Yuasa, Tomoki Hotta, Junko Rodriguez, Sota Torigoe, and Kanae Ervin who were extremely insightful and encouraging.

I also would like to say thank you to all of you readers around the world from the core of my heart. I wish you enjoy this book and find a deep connection with the real you.

You are more than You.

Faithfully,

Rieko Sasaki